DARPA

GENESIS

Vol. I

MANUEL PELAEZ

Darpa Genesis by Manuel Pelaez

ISBN 978-1-952027-92-5 (Paperback)
ISBN 978-1-952027-93-2 (Hardback)

This book is written to provide information and motivation to readers. Its purpose is not to render any type of psychological, legal, or professional advice of any kind. The content is the sole opinion and expression of the author, and not necessarily that of the publisher.

Printed in the United States of America.

New Leaf Media, LLC
175 S. 3rd Street, Suite 200
Columbus, OH 43215
www.thenewleafmedia.com

THE
PROJECT

INTRODUCTION

My novels contain all my knowledge and wisdom from my previous complicated projects, bringing that experience into the transition of writing novels, giving each novel many parts, many twist and turns, giving adventure, sci-fi, suspense, drama, in every book, it is my pleasure to bring you my talents, enjoy Manny Pelaez.

THE CHARACTERS

The Parents of Main Characters
> Natasha – mother
> Will – father

Main Characters
> Terrence
> Marcus
> Father Mike

Sister Nuns
> Sarah, Lucy, Teresa, Joy

Parents of Marcus
> Sylvia – Step Mom
> James – Step Father

Team of Robotic Engineering Scientist
> Marcus, Jou, Roy, Thomas, Jing
> Admiral Thompson
> Agent Jones and CIA Operatives
> Dark Lords
> Ancient Tribal Civilization
> Ray - Church Member
> Zon - Elder Tribal Leader
> Chris Whitman - United States Congressman
> Agent Jones & Special Team

This story is about two brothers growing up in Nigeria, facing the brutal and horrific hold on many countries by the rebels and terrorist groups, their parents were farmers and worked very hard to raise their two sons(Natasha 44 years old, his mother, and Wil 48 years old, his father) were murdered and decapitated by the rebels and terrorist groups, (they along with many others, were caught up in the civil wars, going on in Nigeria at the time, which was a worldwide crisis, even the airport was closed housing thousands of refugees, thousands of Nigerians were murdered by the rebels and terrorist).

One brother Terrence 14 years old, his African name is (soldaat) warrior, and Marcus 13 years old, his African name is (Izem) lion, Terrence was taken by the rebels when he was a young boy, where he was taken to camps along with others to learn how to be a killer, specializing in marksmanship, combat training using all kinds of weapons.

Marcus escaped with a small group of church members to safer parts of Africa, led by father Mike(he started his ministries since he was a young priest, affiliated with other ministries worldwide helping people in many regions)and the sister nuns, Sarah (was good friends with Marcus mom(Natasha) for many years), Lucy, Theresa, and Joy, (the nuns were involved in many missionary efforts worldwide also).

Afterwards, they made arrangements with their other fellow churches, and went to America(escaping the brutality of their homeland at the time, and live in a safer environment)to join with them, assigning Marcus in a good home and part of a family, (Sylvia was his step mom, and James was his step dad, they were both part of the ministries of father Mike).

Marcus flourished in school and sports, having many role models in the churches and its members, with plenty of support he joined the United States Army Corp, playing football in the Army university and getting into the special forces green beret unit.

DARPA
TOP SECRET
PROGRAM

He later earned a scholarship in engineering and entered the DARPA program, (engineering for futuristic super soldiers),being part of a small top secret experimental program.

Composed by small group of robotic engineering scientists which names are Marcus 35 years old, living in the Maryland top secret facility living quarters six months out of the year, has a girlfriend, Julie 32 years old, is a neurologist working in a New York trauma hospital, dating on and off since employed by the federal government, no kids, travels somewhat on vacations, Marcus owns a nice spacious condominium in the New York suburb district, no other relatives known maybe a distant brother which he doesn't know if he's alive, Marcus, enjoys sports mostly basketball, football, skiing, water sports also.

Jou 38 years old, living in Maryland top secret facility living quarters six months out of the year, has a wife Sue, works in the automotive industry Toyota headquarters in Colorado, and daughter Lily, 12, goes to school Silver Springs Academy, he owns a beautiful house in Colorado, Jou, enjoys skiing and natural parks, travels to Japan many times to see his parents Ming mother 80 years old, and Ty his father 85 years old.

Roy 36 years old, living in Maryland top secret facility quarters six months out of the year, has a girlfriend called Joyce 32 years old, works as a veterinarian with her own practice in the Massachusetts area, has a son Billy 14 years old, goes to school in Massachusetts, They own a house in Massachusetts, Roy, enjoys going to Canada to visit his parents Grace 78 years old his mom, and Bill is father 82 years old, going hunting and horseback riding.

Thomas 33 years old, living in Maryland top secret facility quarters six months out of the year, is a bachelor dating multiple women and has a house in Germany where his parents live also, Maureen his mom 77 years old, and his father John 80 years old, Thomas, enjoys swimming, mountain climbing, horseback riding, and racing.

Jing 35 years old, has a wife Lynn 30 years old, works at Jackson Memorial hospital as a surgeon, they have two daughters, Amy 11 years old, goes to school in Coconut Grove Academy, Tayler 10 years old, goes to school in Coconut Grove

Academy also, they own a house in Carol Gables Florida, Jing, enjoys going to museums, zoos, and operas, travels often to Japan to visit his parents, Mia his mother 75 years old, and father Bruce 80 years old.

Their work assignments are deploying robotic soldiers and high-tech drones on top secret missions to many dangerous regions, including Africa, Liberia, Somalia, and other parts, where known terrorist and rebel training camps are located and greatly reduce human soldier causalities.

Terrence went on and grew in the ranks with the rebels and terrorist organizations, he became one of the top leaders, plotting and planning many attacks throughout Africa and other parts.

One day the robotic super soldiers were deployed to engage in a brutal battle in Somalia and parts of Liberia, they were heavily outnumbered.

The rebels and terrorist death toll was high, but a major incident happened, a small village was completely destroyed, everyone in that village were killed, women, children, farm workers, innocent civilians, by the super soldiers, no survivors, only two witnessed this brutal event, Terrence and another member of the rebels fled just in time, unable to say anything because they are enemies of the state, the country, and internationally.

Terrence kills the other member, for this incident to be buried with him, when he goes back to the camps the rebels take refuge in a different location to be out of reach high in the mountains, from the super soldiers, this event was quickly covered up, the village was burned, the dead were torched, and even the bones were taken away, no hard evidence whatsoever, the team of engineering scientists quickly had a gag order imposed on them.

AGENT SMITH
& CIA OPERATIVES

Admiral Thompson, which has been in the United States Army for 35 years earning many medals for his service, he lost his older son in combat, he was in the Army Corp, he never recovered emotionally, which many say drove him crazy and towards being corrupted and heartless.

Admiral Thompson, in secret mobilizes teams of CIA operatives led by agent Smith, to takeout the robotic engineering scientists one by one, making it look like accidents.

Jou, (who was a Japanese robotic engineer scientist since the beginning when the program started), was running in the park, early in the morning, close to his house when a person in a bike road by him and shot him in the head, than entered a van that was waiting a block away.

Roy, (who also started since the robotic engineering program began and went to school in the states, graduating top in his class) was swimming in his pool in the evening, when he was drowned, nothing was found anywhere around the premises or in the pool.

Thomas, (he also started since the robotic engineering program began, he went to school in Germany top of his class), was driving his sports car when his car went off a cliff, a little oil pond was found in the road side where cliffs are located, plunging down the rocky cliff to his death.

Jing, (started since the beginning of the robotic engineering program, and graduated with honors from Japan and America), was found dead on the floor it appears his heart stopped from complications, no witnesses, no noise, very mysterious, when Marcus tried calling his colleagues and there was no answer.

CARGO FREIGHTER SHIP
BATTON

He suspects foul play and went straight to father Mike to help him,(which led many missionaries all over the world, and was Marcus mentor throughout his life), to somehow get him out of the country fast, hiding him as if he was part of missionaries, by boat, (cargo freighter ship named batton), they left to Africa.

Once arriving and with help by the churches there, he was smuggled into Northern Africa, once there he kept a low profile, but that didn't stop the CIA operatives in teams from looking for him, they were gathering intel and waiting for reliable sources to proceed further, and know when to take action.

THE DARK LORDS
DONKERE HERE
AFRICAN WORD

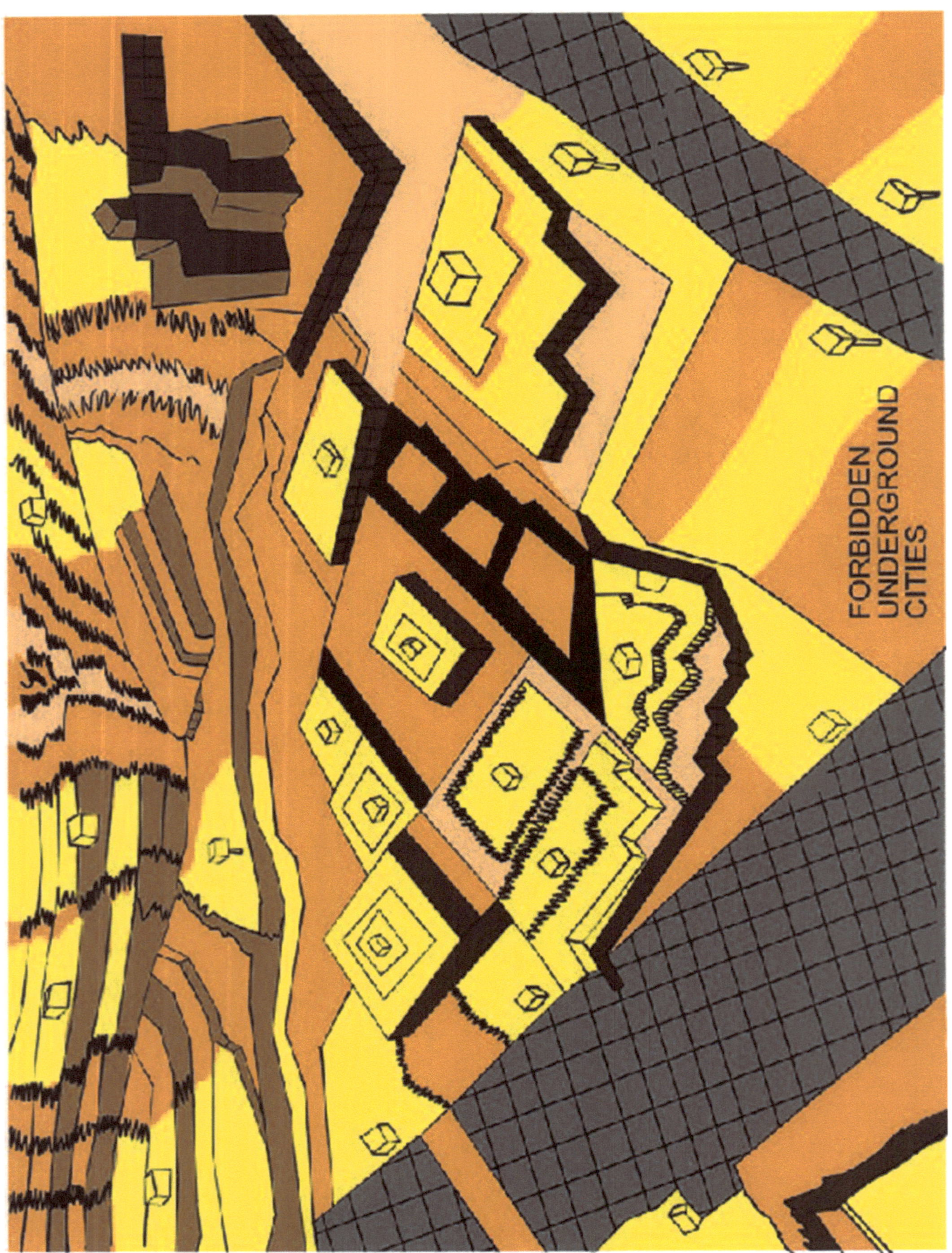

FORBIDDEN
UNDERGROUND
CITIES

(Both Marcus and Terrence when they were small boys heard mystical stories, about some tribal warlords that may have some knowledge in Northern Africa about the dark lords), the African word (donkere here) a mystical group going back centuries,(throughout ancient times, that live in the forbidden cities underground).

When Marcus set off in search of them to hide and remain safe, the church member, (Ray has been with the missionaries in Africa since it started).

Ray, took him as far as he could but both were detained by the rebels and groups of terrorist, lucky for Marcus that Terrence his brother recognized him when they brought them to the camps, they were just in time, because they were about to be executed.

The brothers haven't seen each other since they were teenagers, Marcus explained what was going on, and to allow the church member (Ray)to be free, Terrence said it was ok, but no more communication with the outside world, so the rebels and terrorist appeared to let them go, but assassinated Ray later on, and disappearing any evidence, Marcus had no idea and will never find out, because there is no communication with the outside world whatsoever.

Marcus asked his brother Terrence to help him find the dark lord's.

ZON
ELDER TRIBAL LEADER

Terrence knew of a tribal leader, especially Zon the elder which has been a main leader since the beginning of time and knows something, but Terrence also offered Marcus to Join the cause and be by his side, but Terrence knew his brother only wanted to live in peace because of the organization he was in, and felt horrible about everything. In private the brothers spoke about their memories about growing up, and their parents, Terrence told Marcus that he'll help him, the next day they set off to see the tribal leader, Terrence said his goodbyes and Marcus went with them, when Marcus was alone with the tribal leader they spoke and told him that he will take him to the dark lord's, because he is from pure African descent, and as a favor to Terrence, but he must have his head covered to not know anything about the location, and stay quiet the whole time, only one tribal leader knows how to communicate with the dark lord's.

When they left, and arrived, Zon makes a series of mixed sounds of birds, out of nowhere one comes out, the tribal leader Zon gives Marcus to them, and with it he surrenders what was his old life.

The dark lord's live underground in cities and sustain all their needs by spreading the work details among their groups, the modern world has no recognition of their existence, which dates back many generations in ancient times.

By now the CIA operatives led by agent Smith, (top agent in his class, graduated with honors, and given a supervisory position shortly after the academy, has been given many medals throughout the years), the search intensifies, their given in secret, (by all means necessary to find Marcus).

REBELS AND TERRORIST GROUPS
SOPHISTICATED WEAPONS

The DARPA program continues using militarized drones and other super soldiers,(instead of human soldiers),against the opposition in Somalia and Liberia, but they are outnumbered but still hold their own, the rebels and terrorist groups number in the hundreds of thousands, fierce battles almost everyday, the rebels and terrorist groups have sophisticated weapons and support from other countries, the battles are endless.

By now Marcus is nowhere to be found, but the CIA operatives will never stop searching for him. Agent Smith, and the CIA operatives, are waiting for the right time with accurate intel about where Marcus went in Africa, and more valuable information on when to strike the camp secretly, without causing an international incident.

Back in camp, the other church members know how dangerous it would be going to Northern Africa to find word of Ray,(which was killed when leaving Marcus afterwards), (the other church members think that Ray stayed with Marcus and they found refuge there somehow, and Ray will come back soon).

Back in the states, an investigation has been started, led by Congress, (congressman Chris Whitman, which has been elected consecutively for several years in his district of Maryland) leads to investigate the incidents with the top secret DARPA program super soldiers and high tech drones, and the mysterious deaths of the robotic engineering scientists, plus the disappearance of Marcus, but with hardly any proof or concrete evidence, it's hard to determine what exactly happened on any given date.

A special committee is organized to further collect information or any kind of evidence, special agent Jones from the FBI, leads the assignment, (he has solved numerous crimes, and has a impeccable record going back 20 years.

Back in the battlefields of Africa, Terrence is killed in a raid late at night by advanced military drones equipped with inferred technology, now his secrets are gone forever, the attacks from the rebels and terrorist groups continue throughout Africa.

The superpower nations are having summits to determine how to stop them, combining forces, but trust is a major issue, if somehow they can join forces they have a real chance of defeating the rebels and terrorist groups, if so, this will change the landscape of Africa forever.

In order for this to happen the superpowers must combine their technologies and take risks.

Meanwhile, Marcus is learning and evolving inside the forbidden underground cities, being part of the dark lord's world, workers have assignments daily in groups, and are taught many skills, they are completely self-independent providing everything they need, from energy, the same way as in ancient times, food, water, learned throughout generations.

Meanwhile, (the battles continue for months with many causalities on both sides, the rebels and terrorist are humans equipped with sophisticated weapons, against robotic military super soldiers, and drones, led by other scientists that admiral Thompson assembled), while pending the outcomes of the Congress investigation, (led by congressman Whitman).

At the United Nations many countries vote against the bloodshed and get involved to stop the crisis, to prevent catastrophes, health outbreaks, or the further expansion of civil wars throughout the region from happening, but the superpowers in secret are still trying to build on their trust to create a top secret robotic engineering militarized program that's united, to stop the rebels and terrorist worldwide, but it's still under development, time will tell if the world can come together and create such a overwhelming militarized force composed of robotic super soldiers and state of the art drones, to patrol our world, in every region.

In many world leaders mind, there is the vision of total dominance combining the latest technologies in robotic engineering, high tech drones, hypersonic speeds in aviation, and missiles, pulse weapons, in a one world force, but many see the dangers of that also, because they can use advanced technologies on civilizations to track them better(like identification chip implants, or advanced tracking devices, pretending to make our world safer, but more sinister implications may occur).

In secret, agent Smith has intel about a small group of church members in Africa, from a reliable source informant (Troy), that knows the area well, and has been used before if the money is right.

Agent Smith, gives the order to the CIA operatives in teams to kidnap the church members, pinpointing the camp where Marcus went to, and left with Ray to a location in Northern Africa, the small church group was there, the CIA operatives quickly kipnapped the small group and took them to a unknown location and started torturing them one by one, they were eight in total, to see if anyone knows exactly where Ray took Marcus, after torturing some of them.

One finally knows where Ray took Marcus, and tells them how to get there, they take him with them, and the others were murdered without him knowing anything, leaving no witnesses, after taking the one church member and confirming the location, they kill him also, agent Smith, knows that Marcus is the only person that knows what happened that day in the village where many innocent civilians were accidentally killed and everything was covered up, but in that sector, the rebels and terrorist occupy many territories, finally they get the locations.

They need help from the DARPA top secret robotic engineering program, the new robotic engineer scientists answer directly to admiral Thompson, and both agent Smith and the admiral are good friends, they talk in private, in a secret location off the grid, they discuss how in the hell can we get Marcus in that region and it's located in the heart of rebels and terrorist occupied territories, where Marcus must be hiding there, they both came down with a plan to attack the region in different points, but using drones in high attitudes for information gathering, or enemy conformations, they will use the military robotic super soldiers, and the CIA operatives will assist, the date and time is set.

Now it's wait and see, they are completely outnumbered by the rebels and terrorist, that number in the hundreds of thousands, with advanced weapons, they both come to a agreement, that the attack must be late at night, and quick, kidnapping key enemy soldiers, if possible to interrogate and torture, for any answers on Marcus, the night came, first the drones flew by.

Surveillance from the drones confirm several terrorist and many rebels in the camps, the attack begins, explosions everywhere, thousands of bullets, smoke everywhere, they manage to capture a couple of terrorist and some rebels, before the reinforcements come to the rebels and terrorist fast in the thousands.

The entire squads, and teams, leave and relocate at a secret location.

They start interrogating and torturing the captured rebels and terrorist for information, they told them that Terrence was killed in a raid, and he took Marcus somewhere far away, they pushed more for a location, one said that he just knows in the direction they went, but nothing else.

The next day they took him to point where, in which direction they went, after he pointed, they killed him, and the others back in the secret location, leaving no evidence behind, they disappeared the bodies, cleaned up everything, done by specialized cleaners.

They quickly put together a team of archeologist, trackers, expert hunters, and a team of DARPA military robotic super soldiers, and agent Smith, to see what's out there, what villages, mountains, fields, anything.

In the meantime, Zon the elder tribal leader dies from old age, the only living being on earth with any knowledge of the dark lord's (donkere here) in African, no other tribes, or leaders, know they exist, a spiritual ceremonial funeral was given to Zon, he left behind five children, Ru, Hyp, Shu, Whit, Clay, a great leader, and amazing father, grandfather, his body wrapped around traditional clothes, and the fires were lit, now he goes back to the Kingdom.

From the command center temporary tents, surveillance equipment, portable restrooms, living quarters, and the team went to near by villages, to talk to tribal members, civilians, but knowing that they cannot use force on regular people, because it's way to many innocent civilians, and would cause an international incident worldwide, they all said that they haven't seen Marcus, and don't know where he went, or is living, if alive or dead.

The team decides to do aerial surveillance using drones for months, hoping to record any confirmation on Marcus, they also went to the region to see the territory, the team couldn't find anything, after months pass by, the team concludes that Marcus must have died, or went missing somehow by unnatural causes, but every year we will continue to use aerial surveillance using drones to see what comes up.

The truth of what happened that dreadful day will never be told, or known worldwide for justice to be served, it would have implicated so many powerful people in government, that would have shocked the world.

The investigations will continue in the states, but with no evidence, no witnesses, no one coming forward, it will take a miracle to uncover this extraordinary cover up.

Meanwhile, in the states agent Jones, carefully interviews the family members of the DARPA top secret program.

Surveillance cameras were placed outside the scientists homes without their know how, agent Jones and his team recovered them to be analyzed further at the laboratories, concerning the mysterious deaths of the robotic engineering scientists.

Agent Jones and team also interviewed the neighbors near by, even father Mike, and his ministry, the sister nuns also, and Julie the neurologist that Marcus was dating on and off.

Agent Jones, told his team that this investigation will continue open for as long as it takes, and wherever it takes us, he reports directly to congressman Chris Whitman.

What no one knew, is that the DARPA top secret program robotic engineering scientists, while getting processed in secret had Identification micro size chips implanted in them, under the skin, to track them at all times, even when they are not in the living quarters on base, six months out of the year, not even admiral Thompson which leads the program, or agent Smith, and the CIA operatives, only congressman Chris Whitman knows about the identification micro size implant chips, put in as a safe guard.

When agent Jones reviews the footage it reveals Marcus going to the ministry of father Mike, but Marcus did not use his car, he probably went in a taxi.

Agent Jones orders father Mike to be picked up and interrogated, they set out to the ministry, and take father Mike, to a federal interrogation room in a secret location.

Once there, agent Jones reveals the information he has gathered, and offers father Mike, protective witness program, where he will be safe from any harm, he also asks him if anyone else knows about this, father Mike tells him, that he is the only one that helped Marcus get out of the country, because Marcus was afraid for his life.

Father Mike, tells him everything, the name of the boat, (freighter ship Batton), and where he went in Africa.

Now, agent Jones keeps his word in keeping father Mike safe, by placing him in the federal witness protection program.

Agent Jones takes a team to Africa, going to interview the church members, the team goes in a private jet to Africa.

Once in Africa, agent Jones, and his team, go to the church members church, to interview many of them, and learn about the disappearance of eight church members.

Once agent Jones gathers all the evidence, and the suspicious murders, that took place with the DARPA top secret program, robotic engineering scientists, and the mysterious disappearance of eight church members.

Agent Jones, comes to the conclusion that secret operatives were involved, and somehow, everything is linked to admiral Thompson, which heads the program, and nothing can be done, without his know how.

Agent Jones, gives the order to interrogate admiral Thompson, he must be detained, and question, at all cost.

Meanwhile, agent Jones, comes down to an agreement, with the church members, to place a undercover agent there among them, to see any further activities, by the secret operatives, and the safety, of the church members.

Now we have eyes on Africa, and can monitor things in the region, and hopefully get more intel on Marcus someday, (even though Marcus has a identification micro size chip implant, inside the underground forbidden cities are covered in lead base rock, which enables any tracking abilities).

Back in the states, FBI agents, are trying to have surveillance on admiral Thompson, and wait for the team to arrive from Africa, to detain him.

Agent Smith, and the CIA operatives, notice unusual activities around admiral Thompson.

An operative tells admiral Thompson what was going on, and agent Smith, and the CIA operatives, they dismantle, and flee, to secret locations, to stay hidden from the turmoil.

When agent Jones from the FBI, and his team, arrive in the states, he receives really bad news.

While trying to have eyes on admiral Thompson, and before closing in on him, he shot himself, in the head, using a small caliber handgun.

Admiral Thompson, was in his office at home, and was pronounced dead in the late afternoon.

This infuriates agent Jones, he is so mad that no ones dares to talk to him.

After one hour passes, agent Jones, composes himself, and calls congressman Chris Whitman, to arrange a meeting in private.

Agent Jones, also gives the order to his team to collect everything pertaining to admiral Thompson.

The meeting in private, between agent Jones, and congressman Chris Whitman begins, agent Jones tells him, that all these mysterious events, were done by professional operatives, and clean up crew.

We are currently going through everything, but expect no miracles, all evidence, any links, anything, were probably vanished.

FBI AGENT JONES & SPECIAL TEAM

Agent Jones, request a special team to hunt them down worldwide, anything they can find, including word of secretive operatives, living in remote regions.

Agent Jones, also tells congressman Chris Whitman, that we already have eyes in Africa, and this mission is time consuming.

Congressman Chris Whitman, tells agent Jones, whatever you need, wherever it takes us, as much time it takes, my trust is in your hands wholeheartedly.

Only time will give us more valuable information, and bring closure to the families, of the robotic engineering scientists, the church members, and any further information on Marcus.

THE HUNT
THE PROJECT SEQUEL

INTRODUCTION

In the special world of writing novel books, my mind has evolved and expanded, to bring the creations of characters, worlds, adding drawings to give it life, and favor, to each novel.

It is my pleasure, to see my creations formed in full color, and the stories behind them, enjoy Manny Pelaez.

The Characters

Main Characters

    Marcus

    Julie (The Neurologist)

    Chris Whitman - United States Congressman

    Agent Jones from the FBI

    Special Team

    Military Commandos

    Trackers (Quin)

    Interpol

    The Sniper (Pete)

Region Brazil

    Rouge Agent (Henry Paz Smith)

    Informant (Diego)

Region Agentina & Antartica

    Rouge Agent (Amond Johnson)

    Informant (Jorge)

    Informant (David)

Region Germany

    Rouge Agent (Victor Ramz)

    Agent Vonn - (Cascope) Federal Intelligence Service

Region Taiwan

    Rouge Agent (Lee Hun Sun)

    Taiwanese Secret Service

    Agent (Hann)

    Informant (Len Cho)v

Whit (The late Zon's Son)
Undercover Agent in Africa
The Dark Lord
Robotic Engineering Scientists
Marcus Johnson
Tim Von Gleason
Jon Tan Lan
Sam Andre Dame

AGENT JONES AND SPECIAL TEAM

gent Jones, and his special team composed of military commandos, snipers, the best trackers, Interpol, in the laboratories examining every footage of the surveillance tapes, in reference towards the suspicious murders of the robotic engineering scientists, using high tech facial recognition technologies, they get multiple hits on the individuals involved.

Full profiles of the secretive assassin team involved, the footage tapes reveal four individuals. The first, is the leader of the team, rouge agent Henry Paz Smith who has served in the CIA for over 20 years, and apparently was involved in many shady activities, reporting directly to the late Admiral Thompson, and was in charge of an assassin squad. His last known whereabouts was somewhere in Brazil, he comes from a Brazilian ancestry. The second, is rouge agent Amond Johnson, he has served over 15 years in the CIA, and apparently was involved also in the assassin squad, he fled to Argentina, and somehow went further to Antártica, his relatives always lived in cold regions, he is used to extreme cold temperatures.

The third, is rouge agent Victor Ramz, he served in the CIA for over 13 years, and is originally from the south, he has a half-brother that is involved in the neo-nazi movement, it is believed he fled to Germany, to be part of that movement, seeking protection and shelter. The fourth, rouge agent Lee Hun Sun, his ancestry is from Asia, having relatives in Taiwan, making things very difficult if he somehow crosses the border into China. Agent Jones, and his special team will begin hunting each rouge CIA operative, in corporation with intelligence, and resources from other countries if necessary, The goal is to bring them to justice dead or alive,(the team will be using a small passenger plane in each covert operation, because it doesn't raise suspicion).

Agent Jones, and his special team take off by private small passenger plane to Brazil, to gather intel, and meet with informants living in the region. Once they arrived, they gather together to proceed forward with a plan, the intel on the rouge agent Henry Paz Smith, shows his grandfather is part of a secretive tribal group, that is called the snake people. It is believed that a giant serpent protects them, a native informant (Diego)near the amazon knows of an ancient tribal group that lives deep in the amazon region, the terrain in that region is brutal, mostly heavy jungle, full of dangerous insects, snakes, predators, no vehicles can enter. The plan is to go with a small team, including the native, and get as close as possible to the snake people, in total silence, and stealth. Many miles inside the amazon, in a unknown location the team sets up camp, completely camouflaged, they will use small drone birds, and drone insects, for surveillance, almost invisible to the human eye, because they look extremely life like.

The team will be there as long as possible, until confirmation is detected, then a sniper (Pete)will take position at a 1000 yards, or slightly less, after the kill shot to the head. The entire team will mobilize to a clearing nearby, the river is close by, where they can board a combat rubber raiding craft boat (CRRC)with outboard engine, and travel up river, to the destination, where land transport is waiting, so they can go to the air field and finally leave by plane out of the region. This plan doesn't harm the local natives and eliminates any international incident from occurring.

SNAKE TRIBAL VILLAGERS

At the camp deep inside the amazon, they launch the insect, and bird drones, months past until finally they get surveillance confirmation on the rouge agent Henry Paz Smith, the snake people snake tattoos, and snake skin as clothing, there is even a snake statue curved in stone. The team takes their positions, the sniper gets into his post, early that morning the drones signal confirmation, and went back to camp. The sniper (Pete) gets in position, sees the target, aims, fires, a clear shot to the head. Back at camp, out of nowhere, a giant serpent comes out from the heavy jungle attacking the native informant (Diego), and the tracker (Quin)) killing them both, and swallowing them whole.

The rest of the team opens fire, and uses grenades on the giant serpent, the serpent moves into the hidden jungle, wounded but alive. The team mobilizes quickly before they encounter hundreds of snake tribal groups, the sniper (Pete) joins them, and they set off with their bags, heading towards the river close by to board combat rubber raiding craft boat (CRRC)with outboard engine. The team is professional, and even though the events were dramatic, they must continue the mission, the myths were true about a giant serpent that protects it's people. The team reaches the Jeep, and proceeds on land towards the airfield. The team quickly boards the small passenger plane, and leaves the region quietly, once inside the small passenger plane, witnesses share what they saw, the giant serpent must have been over 60 feet in length, many say it must have been a giant black anaconda.

They lost a valuable member of the team, (Quin was an excellent tracker, and the native informant (Diego), that helped them with the location). Back in the states, Agent Jones gives Congressman Chris Whitman a full report on the first mission, and request another tracker to replace (Quin), in the report agent Jones explains it was impossible to bring the rouge agent Henry Paz Smith alive, because he was protected by hundreds of ancient snake people with weapons, no villagers were harmed, and it was a clean kill. The team will go to Argentina first to gather with a reliable informant there, to determine exactly where the rouge agent Amond Johnson fled to. If he fled to Antártica, the team needs reliable contact informants in Antártica, the plan is for the team to join scientists there living in science stations, where they can assess the intel, and proceed forward.

We will try our best to take the rouge agent Amond Johnson alive by using tranquilizers, creating a diversion, a minor explosion, and sled him out quickly, we will be using snow mobiles, and only have windows of opportunities to act due to the severe weather. Agent Jones, and the special team sets off to Argentina by small passenger plane, once they arrive, they gather with a reliable informant called Jorge. Jorge explains to the team that the rouge agent Amond Johnson has family here, and they live close to the mountains, but set off to Antártica to blend in with scientists living in science stations, one scientist is close to the the rouge agent Amond Johnson's family. Everything in Antártica is based on latitude and longitude, the science stations are numbered. Agent Jones, and the special team sets off to Antártica to meet with a reliable informant(David), to settle inside a science station, and wait for the right time, and moment, gathering intel, using special cameras with facial recognition hardware, once conformation is made we proceed forward. After months passed by, and daily surveillance, they finally get a confirmation detection on the camera, the team mobilizes in snow mobiles, the season has snow, but not the brutal winter where everything is immobilized due to the severe weather, we go in and out.

Once the team arrives, they quickly plant the small devices to explode on timers, and are in position to enter after the explosions, the devices explode in a timely manner. The team enters in different locations, some machine gun fire is exchanged with the rouge agent Amond Johnson, a combination of tranquilizers, and bullets hitting his legs, he drops to the floor, the team also exchanges gunfire with another person, killing him instantly. It is believed that the other individual in the gunfire was the family friend that was a scientist, that helped him settle in Antártica. The team quickly leaves under all the chaos, the rouge agent Amond Johnson was placed in a weatherproof body bag and carried out in sled in back of a snow mobile.

PACK OF COMMANDOS

They proceed towards the airfield in a tight pack of snow mobiles, once they board the small passenger plane, the physician on board examines the rouge agent Amond Johnson, and declares him in a state of coma, it is determined that an overdose of tranquilizers effected his brain. Now, the team must place the rouge agent Amond Johnson under observation until he awakens from the coma, to collect vital information. Back in the states, the rouge agent Amond Johnson is placed in a federal hospital where he is under observation until he awakens from the coma. Now, agent Jones, and the special team plans the next mission, going after rouge agent Victor Ramz, going to Germany and uniting with The Federal Intelligence Service (CASCOPE), agent Vonn, (both agents have worked together before), getting intel on that dangerous neo-nazi group. Agent Jones and the special team sets off to Germany in the small passenger plane, once they arrive, they go to a secret location with The Federal Intelligence Service, to plan and execute a strategy. Agent Vonn, from the Federal Intelligence Service tells the team that the neo-nazi group are several hundred strong, they are a brotherhood, and are extremely well armed. Agent Vonn continues to say that they have intel that the group is planning a convoy to eastern Ukraine, to assist in the fighting against the Russian separatists, which have murdered over 10,000 thousand countrymen.

The plan is to get facial conformation on rouge agent Victor Ramz, using hidden cameras around their compound, then see exactly what vehicle he will be in, than deploy a micro size bug drone, detaching a magnet GPS tracker to pinpoint the vehicle at all times, than the helicopter can launch a precision small missile from the sky, to avoid engaging in a major firefight with the neo-nazi group and causalities. The plan will minimize war in the streets, fly by hitting the target, and leaving fast, the helicopter will be unmarked, they agree that the plan is the most effective way, because taking him alive is almost impossible without a war in the streets. The team's setup surveillance cameras hidden around the compound, camouflaged like rocks, and are stationed nearby to monitor everything, waiting for the right time and date to execute the plan. After months passed by, the teams finally get a facial recognition detection from the hidden cameras. The neo-nazi groups mobilize the convoy, heading out in vehicles towards eastern Ukraine. The teams get conformation that rouge agent Victor Ramz, has entered vehicle number four, he is with a small group of four, out of forty vehicles, the neo-nazi groups have weapons, rocket launchers, machine guns, grenades.

The plan is to launch a small surface to surface missile on the side where rouge agent is seated, hit and run, before the convoy can take action using the rocket launchers.

When the convoy rolls out,(the convoy is taking the route through Slovakia to enter Ukraine, making things easier for a covert air strike, because their Air Force is limited), the plan is to keep surveillance by land close by without being detected monitoring the vehicle with the gps tracker, the helicopter will strike(inside Slovakia territory)a couple of miles from the border of eastern Ukraine, to keep a safe distance from the anti-aircraft weaponry that is in place in eastern Ukraine, an attack closer to the border makes it easier to blame on the Russian separatists, since the helicopter is unmarked making it impossible to determine the origin, the teams give the signal to the pilot for the aerial assault. The helicopter flies by in stealth mode, the pilot also is monitoring the vehicle using gps tracking software inside the cockpit, and knows that rouge agent Victor Ramz is driving vehicle number four, the helicopter makes it's decent, and launches the surface to surface missile, the precision is extremely accurate. The small surface to surface missile hits the driver's side directly, causing an explosion and killing rouge agent Victor Ramz instantly, the Jeep itself is immobilized completely, others are killed also in the vehicle. By the time the convoy gets out the rocket launchers, the helicopter is gone, out of reach, it seems that the passenger next to the driver was killed, and the passenger seated directly in the back was killed also, only one survivor in the aerial assault.

Most of the neo-nazi group members are considered extremely dangerous, criminal histories, and do everything underground black market, they are a brotherhood, and are militant contractors. This mission was the only way of taking out rouge agent Victor Ramz, and overall the mission was a success, the blame can be linked to the Russian separatists, using a rouge helicopter to disrupt the convoy. The helicopter goes back to camp, safely and secure without incident, some covert missions are complicated, and require joint operations, do to the complexity of dangerous groups, and minimize the causalities. After the covert operation in Germany, the team quickly leaves and sets off by small passenger plane, for the next mission in Taiwan, where agent Jones, and the special team, will gather in a secret location with the National Security Bureau (Taiwanese Secret Service), agent Hann,(both agents have worked on previous assignments before), to see what intel they have on rouge agent Lee Hun Sun, and his exact whereabouts, if any. When landing in Taiwan, The MSS (The Ministry of State Security) The Chinese Secret Service, has surveillance on them already an extremely secretive agency, by far this will be the hardest mission yet. The National Security Bureau (Taiwanese Secret

Service), led by agent Hann, he tells the team that rouge agent Lee Hun Sun has family here in a village by the mountains, and using an informant Len Cho, tells agent Hann, that his last known whereabouts were from a fishing vessel called (Lung Ching), that was part of a group of commercial fishing vessels named(Lee Tun, Yong Ho, Tung Chu, J Lang), which is a live aboard commercial fishing vessel, that stays out months at a time in the high seas.

The Chinese military vessels patrol the Chinese territorial waters very affective, and to have any changes of getting close to those ships must be well planned, with minimal risks, and quick, and outside of those waters. The plan is to go with the informant Len Cho to Lucan Island, it's part of the Philippines, he has connections there to get was is needed, like an unmarked fishing vessel. Agent Jones, and the special team leave with Len Cho the informant, to Lucan Island, the team has everything they need, one of the team is a maritime captain. They land in Lucan Island, and quickly get the unmarked fishing vessel, load the gear they need, three combat rubber raiding crafts(CRRC), small military tactical infrared drones, magnetic tracking sensors with remote release, gas masks, sleeping gas canisters(Oneirogenic General Anaesthetic)(Incapacitating Agent), automatic weapons with silencers, tranquilizers, infrared night gear, ropes, and other equipment. The last known whereabouts of the group of commercial fishing vessels was many miles out at sea, close to Chinese territorial waters, but not exactly in territorial waters, given by agent Hann, from the National Security Bureau (Taiwanese Secret Service), in latitude and longitude.

The plan is get close to the group of commercial fishing vessels, outside Chinese territorial waters, and go late at night in three teams, in three combat rubber raiding crafts, with outboard engines, 100 feet from the group turn off the outboard engines, and paddle the rest of the way, planting magnetic trackers on each ship, above the floating line marker of the ships. Agent Hann is given assurance that the covert operation will be quick and precise, without causing an international incident, or unnecessary harm to the rest of the fishermen.

After weeks passed by, the team approaches the group of commercial fishing vessels, and wait for nightfall, around 2:30am, they launch three combat rubber raiding crafts(CRRC), with teams, 100 feet from the group of ships they turn off the outboard engines, and paddle the rest of the way. They quickly approach the ships and split up the teams, each team attaches magnetic trackers to each ship in total silence, the plan goes well, and they paddle 100 feet away to start the outboard engines, to head towards the unmarked fishing vessel faster. Once, the teams arrive to their unmarked fishing vessel, they can monitor the group of commercial fishing vessels, and wait until they are more out to sea, miles away from Chinese territorial waters. They can follow miles away monitoring the ships, even pinpoint the commercial fishing vessel (Lung Ching), waiting for the right time and moment, to get closer late at night. Launching a military infrared drone in total silence, to attach micro size surveillance cameras on deck of each ship, close to the sleeping quarters, and using facial recognition technology.

Once, they make a positive facial recognition on rouge agent Lee Hun Sun, they can quickly launch a covert operation late at night, boarding the ship, entering the sleeping quarters firing sleeping gas in canisters, while the fishermen are asleep, making visual recognition and apprehend the fugitive rouge agent. Placing him in a weatherproof body bag, with a harness to lower him to the combat rubber raiding craft(CRRC), entering the ocean at night is too risky do to shark infested waters, known to follow commercial fishing vessels. Once, the group of commercial fishing vessels are in the high seas, far away from Chinese territorial waters, the unmarked fishing vessel follows from a distance, later that night, around 2:30am, the unmarked fishing vessel gets closer. To position the vessel to launch the military small tactical infrared drone, in stealth mode, carrying micro size magnetic trackers. The drone flies in total silence and is maneuvered by an experienced operator on board the unmarked fishing vessel, it flies over the dock of each ship, attaching a micro size magnetic surveillance tracker, near the sleeping quarters of each ship.

The micro size tracker is very small hardly noticeable, it is equipped with facial recognition technology. The drone returns to the unmarked fishing vessel without any incident, now it's a waiting game, once facial confirmation is made, the operation will take place later on that night. Days pass by, when the team finally gets facial confirmation on rouge agent Lee Hun Sun, he is on board the (J Lang), this plan is well executed using technology to make this operation successful.

J Lang
COVERT OPERATION

Later on that night, (it was pouring rain, and the seas were a bit rough), around 2:50am, the team launches three combat rubber raiding crafts, with a team of three in each craft, arriving quickly and boarding the (J Lang), in total silence. The teams position themselves, entering the sleeping quarters and firing the sleeping gas (Oneirogenic General Anaesthetic) (Incapacitating Agent) in canisters, the smoke quickly fills the quarters. The teams in gas masks, quickly identifies rouge agent Lee Hun Sun, and quickly puts him in a body bag with harness wrapped around his body completely secured, they quickly carrying him and lower him using ropes, into the combat rubber raiding craft(CRRC), to a team waiting below. The other teams lower down to the crafts, paddling out 100 feet away to start outboard engines, to not make any noise, they also release the other magnetic trackers on the other ships by using a remote switch (not leaving any evidence).

The teams quickly return to the unmarked fishing vessel without incident under heavy rain, boarding the ship with their gear, boats, and the rouge agent, then navigating towards Lucan Island in the Philippines, where they can board the small passenger plane waiting for them, to go back to the states. Overall, the plan went well, by avoiding Chinese territorial waters, and any military vessels in the region, being patient and planting the micro size surveillance cameras made all the difference, pinpointing the exact vessel the rouge agent was on. Once, they arrive at Lucan Island in the Philippines, the teams quickly get in jeeps, and drive towards the airfield to board the small passenger plane, rouge agent is completely subdued, and medicated. Arriving at the airfield, the teams board the small passenger plane with gear, boats, and rouge agent Lee Hun Sun, not leaving any evidence anywhere. They take off to the states, where agent Jones, will turn in a full report in detail of each covert operation directly to Congressman Chris Whitman. Landing back in the states, rouge agent Lee Hun Sun is taken to a secret location to be interrogated and given different drugs to confess his knowledge of incidents that occurred, under the command of the late admiral Thompson. Agent Jones, and the special team, find out later on that day that the other rouge agent Amond Johnson died of complications while in a coma, the doctors tried their best but couldn't save him.

Now, more than ever it's up to specialized doctors to abstract vital information from rouge agent Lee Hun Sun, using the latest drugs. The rouge agent is under heavy medicated drugs to induce information from him, after many hours, each day, weeks go by, and the specialized doctors get vital information from the rouge agent. Learning that the late admiral Thompson put together a squad and ordered the untimely deaths of the robotic engineering scientists, and eight church members in Africa. Led by rouge agent Smith, they were after the scientist Marcus also, but couldn't find out where he disappeared to, ever since, Marcus disappeared, Julie his girlfriend on and off for years, has been repeatedly calling the congressman office to see if any new information has been revealed. Afterwards, gathering all the information, and after agent Jones turns in his reports to Congressman Chris Whitman, they both make plans on how to move forward. Rouge agent Lee Hun Sun is spared the death penalty and will be facing consecutive life sentences in a federal prison, mostly for his vital intel.

The plan now is get Julie involved the neurologist from the trauma hospital in New York,(girlfriend of Marcus, on and off for years), sending her to gather with the undercover agent that has lived among the church members in Africa, both of them can somehow talk to the tribal leaders,(spending a couple of months if necessary), to get the word out that everything is safe now for Marcus. The undercover agent, and Julie, will visit tribal leaders nearby, little do they know, that the children of the late elder tribal leader Zon are among some of the tribes.

They are not aware, that the five children of Zon,(Clay, Shu, Ru, Hyp, Whit), one was given the secret from their father Zon(like in generations of his bloodline), taught how to communicate with the dark lord's, and given their location, this practice goes back since ancient times. Julie, brings with her, several hand written letters by her, which Marcus knows her writing, plus pictures of her, and authentic signatures of the Congressman Chris Whitman, explaining how the threat to Marcus has been eliminated, and how the congressman plans on making a futuristic robotic engineering program better with Marcus's leadership. Julie boards the small passenger plane, bringing with her only the letters, and pictures, the tribes do not trust any electronic devices at all, including cellphones, laptops, etc. In this personal operation, agent Jones, and the special team, do not go, only Julie will gather with the undercover agent, that's among the church members. When the small passenger plane lands in Africa, at a air field close to the church members camp, she goes with the undercover agent that was awaiting her arrival, to the camp to be introduced to the other church members, once she settles in, they will go to each village to speak to the tribes, and drop off the letters and pictures, to somehow reach Marcus.

They leave early in the morning, this region of Africa is safe, but the undercover agent is armed, they go to each tribal village and speak to the elders dropping off the letters and pictures, explaining everything, and telling them that they are close by in the camp with the church members. Marcus will decide how to meet Julie, that part is explained carefully. Now, it's a waiting game, the word will spread and hopefully they will send notice to Julie. While visiting the tribal villages, Whit, one of the late Zon sons, takes notice in Julie's sincerity, seeing her eyes, and emotions, once they leave the village. Whit sets off later that day, in the darkness of night to communicate with the dark lord's, and give them the letters, and pictures, but after carefully examining each paper. Whit is the one chosen by his late father Zon, to have the knowledge of the dark lord's. Through many generations of time, one Zon bloodline has been given the secrets of the dark lord's, going back in ancient times. Whit, carefully arrives and makes a series of bird and animal noises, afterwards, out of nowhere, a dark lord reveals himself. Whit gives him the letters, and pictures, that Julie dropped off in the village, and explained it is for Marcus, the dark lord leaves with the letters, and pictures.

THE DARK LORDS
DONKERE HERE
AFRICAN WORD

FORBIDDEN
UNDERGROUND
CITIES

After disappearing into the darkness, the dark lord returns to the forbidden underground cities, and gives Marcus the letters, and pictures, that Whit gave him, Whit returns to the village under the night darkness. Marcus, in privacy reads the letters carefully, and sees the pictures, he gets emotional, tears are dropping from his face, it is noticeable that he misses Julie, his step parents, father mike, the sister nuns, and the life he left under life threatening situations. After some time passes, the chief tribal leader from the dark lord's, sits down with Marcus, and they have a long conversation about everything. They both agree that if conditions are safe, and Marcus can return without any threatening situations, he can go to the camp where Whit is at, late at night, and only with the village hiding him, the villagers can send someone for Julie. Only Julie will be notified and return to the village under the night darkness with some villagers, Marcus will be waiting hidden. At 2:30am the villagers reach Julie in total silence, and they leave to the village in the night darkness. When they arrive at the village, Julie doesn't have any electronics on her, she is checked carefully by a female villager, at the church camp she changes clothes to be dressed in a custom tribal wear, leaving her clothes back at the church camp. Out of nowhere Marcus unites with Julie in private inside the village, they both hug, and cry, and stay talking about everything that has happened. Julie assures Marcus, that the threat has been eliminated, and he can return with her, to be given great opportunities, leading the DARPA top secret robotic engineering program, with other specialized scientists, for future operations. Marcus agrees, and returns with Julie, boarding the small passenger plane, and returning to the states, the undercover agent stays in Africa with the church members to monitor the rebels and terrorist threats in the region. The small passenger plane returns to the states, and a reunion is done in private, where Marcus is given a medal of service, and meets Congressman Chris Whitman, agent Jones, and the other scientists that he will lead in future operations.

They also discuss the events that occurred, making plans to pay his respect to the murdered scientists from the past, and visit their families, pay a visit to father Mike, the sister nuns, visit his stepparents. Congressman, Chris Whitman goes on to say, we will do are best to normalize everything as long as it takes, and assemble a better DARPA top secret program, with the latest in engineering, technologies, it will be the pride of our accomplishments. We learn from our mistakes, and try to reach perfection, putting robotics and high-tech drones, rather then human lives.

In private, between the congressman, agent Jones, and Marcus, discuss the event that occurred in Africa, where the super soldiers, made the mistake of killing a village of innocent civilians, mistaking them for rebels, and terrorist.

That region of Africa is hostile, and the super soldiers, where engaged in intense battles almost everyday, that incident led to the mysterious murders of the scientists, and forced Marcus to disappear, and the murders of the church members also in Africa. They all agreed, that the DARPA top secret program can continue, but only with new safeguards, and new precautions, must be in place, for these incidents not to occur ever again. They continued agreeing, that the DARPA top secret program, will bring in state of the art technologies, and scientists, including space pioneer developments.

JON
TAN
LAN

SAM
ANDRE
DAME

MARCUS
JOHNSON

TIM
VON
GLEASON

RON
BEN
RUCKMAN

The new team of the DARPA top secret program will include five members, they will range from robotic engineering scientists, space exploration scientists, military mechanical engineers, weapon engineering scientists, led by Marcus Johnson, Tim Von Gleason, Jon Tan Lan, Sam Andre Dame, Ron Ben Ruckman. The team shall live six months in a top-secret facilities, that includes every comfort, completely isolated from civilization, than six months with their families, with security details, the purpose of their jobs is to spare human soldier lives.

THE

PROGRAM

TRILOGY TO THE PROJECT AND THE HUNT

INTRODUCTION

Myself and many others, salute with our hearts, the magical world of literature, it is my great pleasure, to bring you, action, suspense, sci-fi , romance, adventure, drama, a sense of creativity, that's in a world of the beyond, my action novel books, a powerful trilogy and possibly more, (THE PROJECT), (THE HUNT), (THE PROGRAM), with future projects in the works, all made possible by the special world of literature, thank you with all my heart, by Manny Pelaez.

THE CHARACTERS

Congressman Chris Whitman
Director Jones CIA Headquarters

Special Team
    Jeff, Goro, Earnest, Leon, Finn, Charles, Steven, Samuel, and Darryl
    The Sniper Pete
    Interpol Agent Meng
    Marcus Johnson – Main Character
    Julie – The Neurologist
    Father Mike
    Sister Nuns
    Julie's Parent
    Marcus Stepparents
    The Robotic Engineer Scientists
    Marcus Johnson, Jon Tan Lan, Sam Andre Dame, Tim Von Gleason, Ron Ben Ruckman
    Military Strategist and Experts

A new beginning, with extremely complex challenges, in hostile war driven nations, complex social structures, especially in many borders, awakes the team of the robotic engineering program.

The first thing on the schedule is the congressional ceremony to hand out medals and promotions, to agent Jones from the FBI, and the special team that was assembled for each mission.

Going to extreme regions, and planning covert operations, with help from other agencies, and informants.

The congressional ceremony date is set, everybody will be in attendance.

The families of the previous robotic engineering scientists will be in attendance also.

Marcus decides to announce a huge surprise, he and Julie will be getting married as well.

After the congressional ceremony, the next day everyone will gather at his wedding, that will take place in Maryland, where the congressional ceremony will be also.

Marcus plans to invite father Mike, the sister nuns, Julie's parents, his stepparents, the new robotic engineering program scientists, of course, agent Jones, Congressman Chris Whitman, these ceremonial celebrations will be a two-day event, plus another day for the honeymoon. After so many events happened, finally some peace of mind, and happiness.

The preparations are being made, the congressional ceremony will be on Friday morning, an all-day event, the speeches from every individual will be spectacular.

A catering service will bring in the food afterwards, and drinks, it's an event to recognize the bravery, and courage, of everyone involved.

Prestigious medals will be given, promotions will be rewarded.

The wedding itself, will be Saturday morning, with plenty of flowers everywhere, the gathering of friendships, colleagues, families, and the beginning of futures to come.

The day of the congressional ceremony, a military parade performs first, then the firing of rifles from our finest military personnel.

The first to take the stage is Congressman Chris Whitman, he will be the first to speak, agent Jones, and his special team come up stage to be announced.

Everyone bows their head down in a moment of silence to honor the deaths of the previous robotic engineering scientists, Jou, Roy, Thomas, Jing, (their families were compensated financially, and their children were given educational scholarships), the two brave men that were killed in Brazil by the giant serpent deep in the Amazon, our team member and excellent tracker Quin, and the informant Diego, that made everything possible with precious intel, the eight church members in Africa, the village that the terrible incident happened were remembered as well.

The special team nine commandos, which names are, Jeff, Goro, Ernest, Leon, Finn, Charles, Steven, Samuel, and Darryl. The sniper, Pete, and Interpol agent, Meng, which is also a boating caption.

Are each given a medal of valor, and are given promotions in their respected sectors, some are given incentives like early retirement packages if they want.

Agent Jones, is promoted to the director of the CIA headquarters, which under his leadership, that agency can put the past behind them, and bring about a proud agency for futures to come.

Marcus, gets up on stage, and gives a heart warming speech, and tells everyone how the program will be much better, with more sophisticated safe guards, and outstanding colleagues, for futures to come, he is given a medal of valor also, for participating in the program, and coming back to improve it.

The big day is tomorrow for him, and everyone is there, a day of celebrations, and happiness, everybody will be in attendance early the next morning.

The next day, at the church, Marcus and Julie are standing in front of the priest, everyone is in attendance, the entire church is full of fresh flowers, after the vows are given.

Everyone joins in the festival, the reception, a new day has come, the beginning of things to come, everyone is having fun, the conversations are everywhere.

Afterwards, Marcus and Julie, will go on their honeymoon, and relax, have fun, and soon, Marcus will join the new team of robotic engineering scientists, with military personnel, and Congressmen Chris Whitman, to go over the first monumental task.

After a week passes, and everyone is already settled, the team will arrive at the top secret facility, where everyone will join together to begin briefing, planning, strategies, and go over the latest technologies.

The robotic engineering scientists team arrives, they will be here for six months, they are joined by military experts, and military generals.

The discussions begin, let's put everything on the table, the assignment is Afghanistan, the problems are the Durand line, drawn up by the British in 1893, 2,500 km (1.500 plus miles), and the Helmand river water treaty signed by Iran and Afghanistan in March 13, 1973, Afghan Taliban, Pakistani tribal areas, the Islamic State, merchant and humanitarian crisis.

The Pakistan military has already built a barrier fence and have thousands of soldiers protecting its territories, and Iran and Afghanistan are in heated battles over water rights in the Helmand river, which developments for hydro projects are on the way.

Discussions will be the solutions to these ongoing problems, and the composite of the latest medals to make the armor in our robotic super soldiers, and high tech drones, the latest weaponry we can use, and most important, the latest technologies in security systems to secure border walls, and fencing.

Let's begin with the border problems, we can use high energy laser towers (HEL), every 1000 to 2000 feet apart, using an invisible web of laser sensors interconnected beam network, throughout the existing barrier fence that the Pakistan military build, aerial spider drones shall be on standby, with ground super soldiers in storage units nearby.

This entire network can detect anything, a buffer zone of 50 to 75 feet will be placed as a safeguard, anything that comes within the buffer zone, will be eliminated.

The aerial spider drones are equipped with powerful lasers and can have ground and aerial assaults. Check points will be placed in design locations, where food trade, and other merchant trade can occur, trading can only occur at the border, no crossing into Pakistan.

The checkpoints shall have certain times, and days, designated by the Pakistan military, all merchandise shall be moved by cargo transport trucks, driven by Pakistan military on their side, and the Afghanistan government on the other side.

These agreements shall be between all nations involved, this technology shall be used on the entire Durand line, which extends over 2,500 km (1,500 plus miles).

Another major problem is the Iran-Afghanistan border, there is a 3ft thick and 10 feet high concrete wall in place, the border is 700 km (434.96 miles).

We will look into what's needed there, maybe a barrier fence on the side of Afghanistan, and have high energy laser towers (HEL), stationed 1000 to 2000 feet apart, using the invisible web of laser sensors interconnected beam network, and have buffer zones.

The Helmand River is an enormous problem do to climate change and droughts, it is causing major problems with the treaty of March 13, 1973, the water supply in Afghanistan parts is drying up, and Iran has more access to water supply.

A team of engineers will tackle this problem, by becoming HydroHegemon, the hydro dams shall be placed on all three river basins, The Amu Darya, The Kabul, and The Helmand, after this is done, both sides should have plenty of water, the restoration plan, (UNDP) with agreements from Iran and Afghanistan to insure the future of the Helmand River, increasing from 17 BCM to 30 BCM.

The security zones, shall be guarded by some high energy laser towers (HEL), and the spider drones in the buffer zones only, especially at the Kajaki Dam, and Sorobi Dam.

Agreements shall be done among all nations involved, and outside assistance, providing the technologies to solve global problems.

Rumors have it, that Iran is against the Hydro Dam projects, and pays Taliban fighters to sabotage any advancements, the high energy laser towers (HEL), using the spider drones can keep them in check.

Now next on the agenda, is the latest medals used in lightweight composite armor, and latest high technologies in weaponry, that will be designed in our engineering of robotic super soldiers, the drones must be much lighter.

The latest medals for lightweight composite armor known are, Chobham armor, Dorchester armor, Silicon Carbide tiles, we have other formulas to strengthen these known elements.

Next, is the weaponry known up to now, major advancements in the field of electrically powered weapons, rail guns, electromagnets to accelerate a solid slug to supersonic speeds, which is firing pure energy at light speeds, 150 kilowatt lasers.

Major advancements in laser kilowatt technologies, will be used in engineering robotic super soldiers, and drones.

We plan on having individual military storage units that are run by our sophisticated latest militarized robotic super soldiers, and drones, with many safeguards in place, these military storage units shall be placed in Afghanistan, close to borders, and tactical locations, with buffer zones in place around the storage units.

It shall be guarded around the clock, by our super soldiers, and drones, it shall have high energy laser towers (HEL), in assigned locations, the spider drones are equipped with the latest technologies in weaponry, and the ground super soldiers are well equipped as well.

Agreements shall be made among all nations involved, and even the war lords territories won't be affected, terms and agreements shall be among the tribes, the major issues are border problems, to keep the Taliban and terrorist from crossing over, and setting off bombs.

Pakistan government agrees to a shared percentage financially, Iran are much more reluctant, but some type of agreement is discussed.

The entire program is not to have conflicts with other nations, but to secure border issues, and assist when needed, with Taliban or terrorist activities in their country.

First the production of the robotic super soldiers, and high tech drones begin, the team will be on site for everything to run smoothly, and the teams of engineers will instruct the builders what to do, a series of Hydro Dam projects.

The high energy laser towers (HEL), shall be placed first, with the spider drones guarding them from any Taliban or terrorist attacks.

The team of engineering robotics scientists are expecting the worse confrontations in the beginning, once the system is up and running, the program will be tested, as the world watches, but the minds behind the program, are truly gifted, and the expectations are great.

If this program is a success, it is only the beginning of solving major problems throughout our world, and beyond.

Production begins, now the team of robotic engineering scientists awake their deployment, everything is on the line, but Congressmen Chris Whitman, director Jones of the CIA, military experts, and the entire families and friends, of the robotic engineering scientists, couldn't be more proud of them.

The production of minimal robotic super soldiers, and more of high-tech drones, shall take several weeks, because of the mountainous and rugged terrain throughout Afghanistan. After the production of super soldiers, and high tech drones, are finished, they shall be transported by (USAF)C-5M super galaxy cargo planes with F-22's military fighter jet escorts, landing in Bagram military airfield in Afghanistan, digging drill machines, are loaded also, to install the (HEL) high energy laser towers throughout the borders, to protect the storage units, and to protect the team of engineers at the Helmand River, Th e Amu Darya, Th e Kabul, and The Kajaki Dam, The Sorobi Dam.

The team of robotic engineering scientists, military strategists, and experts shall arrive by military plane also.

The military shall begin loading the enclosed containers onto a convoy of trucks, taking them to assigned locations in Afghanistan, and begin unloading the precious cargo.

This entire process will take months, and it will be guarded carefully, this program if successful, could make a difference in many borders, countries, where civil unrest, and wars are apparent, and solve many problems worldwide.

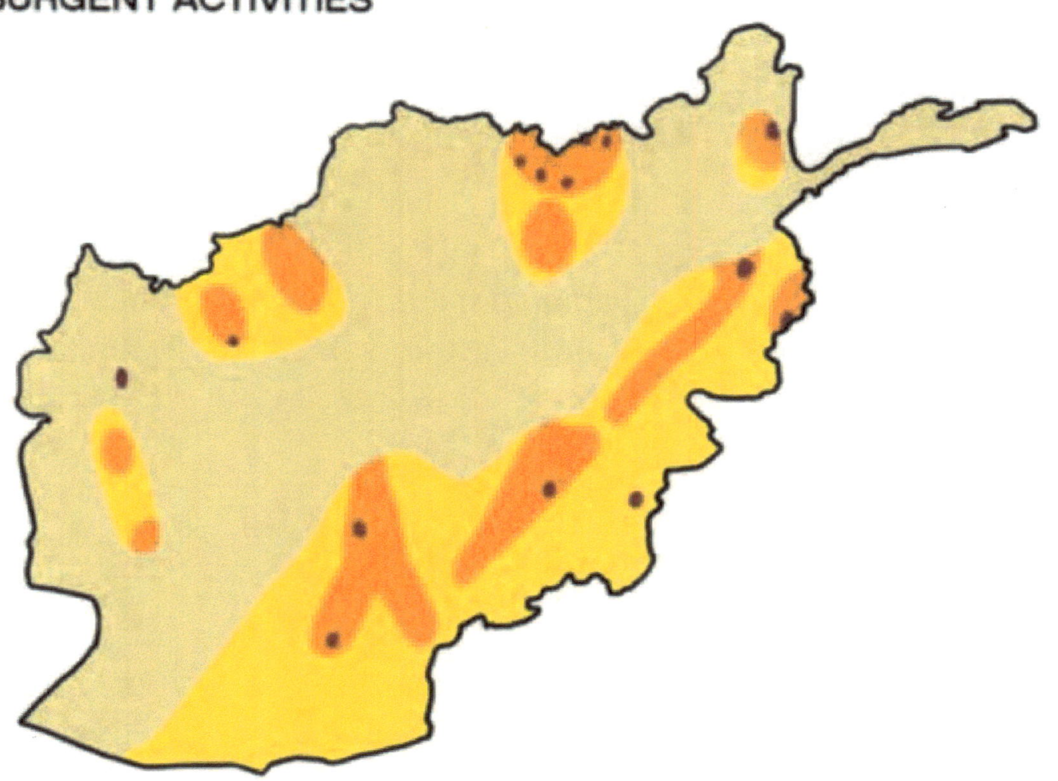

MAP OF AFGHANISTAN
TALIBAN CONTESTED REGIONS
INSURGENT ACTIVITIES

The military strategists, experts, the team of robotic engineering scientists, setup a tent and begin using a map of Afghanistan, showing all the problem areas, where insurgent activities, and Taliban, have been reported, and fighting has occurred.

The individual storage units shall be close by, in tactical locations, equipped with aerial spider drones, and minimal ground robotic super soldiers.We shall place these storage units accordingly to the demand necessary, these aerial spider drones, and robotic super soldiers, are extremely lethal.

The operation begins, and it's precious cargo, the (USAF) C-5M super galaxy cargo planes begin to land, capable of carrying 381T, with a payload of 129,274kg, convoys of trucks load the precious enclosed containers, and head off to the designated areas, with military escorts.

This operation will be on a continuous 24/7 basis, until all the containers are in place.

Since, China is improving and building a military base in Jiwani, and already has a commercial port in Gwadar, Pakistan's western Balochistan province.

In the meantime, at the military tents set up point, the military strategists, expects, and team of robotic engineering scientists, are reviewing the map of Afghanistan, and carefully pinpointing where exactly the storage units should be placed, and distance.

The map shows, the contested regions were insurgents, and Taliban are active, mostly in the north, for instance, the capital of Kunduz, Faryab, Jawzjan, Baghaln, Lashkar, Gah, capital of Helmand, Tarin Kot, province capital of Urozgan province.

The intension of the program is only to engage the insurgents, and Taliban, if assistance is requested by the Afghanistan government, we are however on standby, but the border is are main issue, securing the border, shall prevent terrorist attacks, and save many lives.

The convoy of trucks continue to place containers in designated areas, each container is marked with numbers, and the military is overseeing everything.

The digging machines starts drilling where each (HEL) high energy laser towers, shall be placed, everyone is working on their assignments.

After installing the towers, a kilowatt laser is placed on top, signs are put in place pinpointing the buffer zones, warning markers are visible also, the web interconnected laser network is completely invisible, it can detect anything in the buffer zones, eliminating the threat instantly.

The storage units are placed in areas that are needed, more aerial spider drones, then robotic super soldiers, because of mobility factors.

The entire operation is running smoothly, it will take months to finish, after months go by, everything is in place, the placement of (HEL) high energy towers, include every 2000 feet apart, 2,500kg (1,500 plus miles), in the Pakistan border.

Plus, 700km (434,96 miles), in Iran's border, with another 1,300km (800 miles),along the Helmand River.

The high energy kilowatt lasers are placed on top, and the buffer zones are marked, every tribal leader, citizens, know that it will be active soon, the latest in infrared technologies are part of these lasers.

Agreed by all nations involved, to use these technologies to solve major problems, and prevent future disasters.

If everything goes well, Afghanistan, Pakistan, Iran, shall have the water issues solved, and the constant attacks by Taliban, and insurgents, also terrorist, will reduce greatly.

It has been China's dream, to bring the trans Asian connectivity freight train, a railway with Turkmenistan, and Afghanistan, (one belt), (one road), to bring financial prosperities.

If the program is successful, reforms at the administration level must be apparent, because, corruption, is a major factor, in growth, and prosperity, the lack of proper leadership, Internal differences aside, and bring decisive reforms to the security apparatus.

The program will help bring positive outlook on many hostile areas, and worldwide conflicts, in many regions, most important eliminating human soldier lives.

Finally, the date is set, in one week, the entire system shall be active, each tower shall be armed with (HELL) high energy laser, kilowatt beam.

An invisible web of laser sensors interconnected beam network, with buffer zones, that can detect anything.

The military storage units shall be equipped mostly with aerial spider drones, and minimal ground super soldiers, placed in tactical locations.

The entire areas, shall be watched by space, satellites in orbit, that can monitor large movements from the Taliban, insurgents, terrorist, and deploy the aerial spider drones quickly, and some ground super soldiers if needed.

The (HELL) high energy laser towers can also fire at precise targets, especially in the three large river basins, The Amu Darya, The Kabul, The Helmand, and the dams, Kajaki, Sorobi.

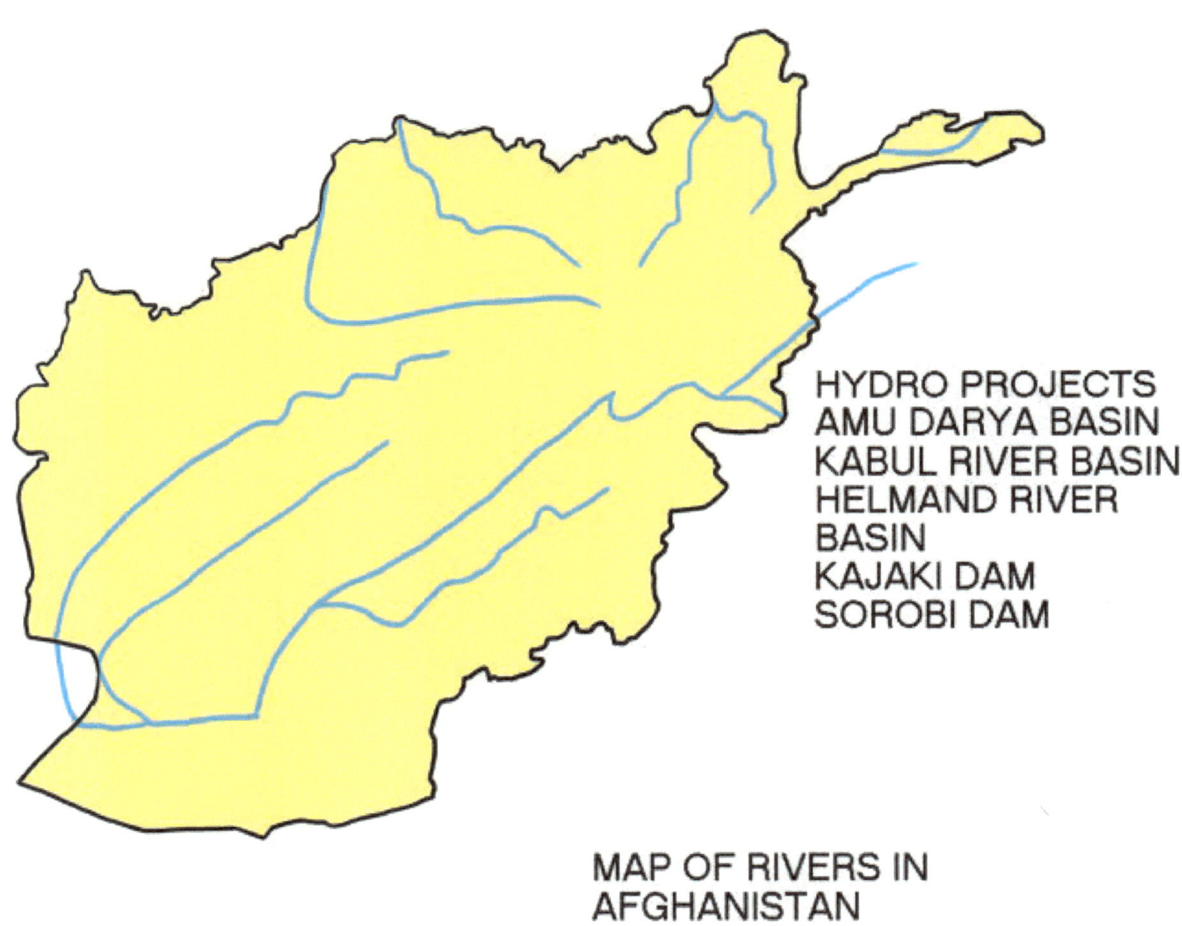

HYDRO PROJECTS
AMU DARYA BASIN
KABUL RIVER BASIN
HELMAND RIVER BASIN
KAJAKI DAM
SOROBI DAM
MAP OF RIVERS IN AFGHANISTAN

Hydro projects, which includes, Hydro Dams, collecting bacterial spores, from water evaporation, turning it into reusable water again, and manufacturing electricity, shall not only increase the BCM from 17 to 30, but also succeeding in Biophysicist, Socioeconomic, Environmental, Hydrologic, challenges for futures to come.

The day has arrived, and the entire system is turned on, everything seems quiet, hours pass by, the team of robotic engineering scientists, military strategists, and experts, are monitoring everything from their base tent camp.

Suddenly, the satellites detect, large numbers of people moving in various locations, in the Kunduz province, across Faryab, Jawzjan, Baghaln, and also in the Helmand province, Lashkar, Gah, even more activities, in the Urozgan province, Tarin Kot.

In the hundreds, maybe thousands, the satellites show even, groups close to the border wall, with heat signatures, like rocket launchers, even (IED) improvised explosive devices.

This is unbelievable, attacks late at night from every position, scores of movements confirm this, and the system only has moments to take action, or be destroyed.

Satélite conformation is given, that all approaching large groups are hostiles, then the roof opens completely on each military storage unit, the aerial spider drones, each platform sides out, when the aerial spider drones take off , the platform hides again.

This entire process, doesn't take long, also the ground super soldiers, roll out, in a different military storage unit, these military storage units that house the super soldiers, are in tactical locations, where the terrain is not as brutal, because of mobility factors.

AERIAL SPIDER DRONE
KILOWATT LASERS
RETRACTABLE SPIDER LEGS

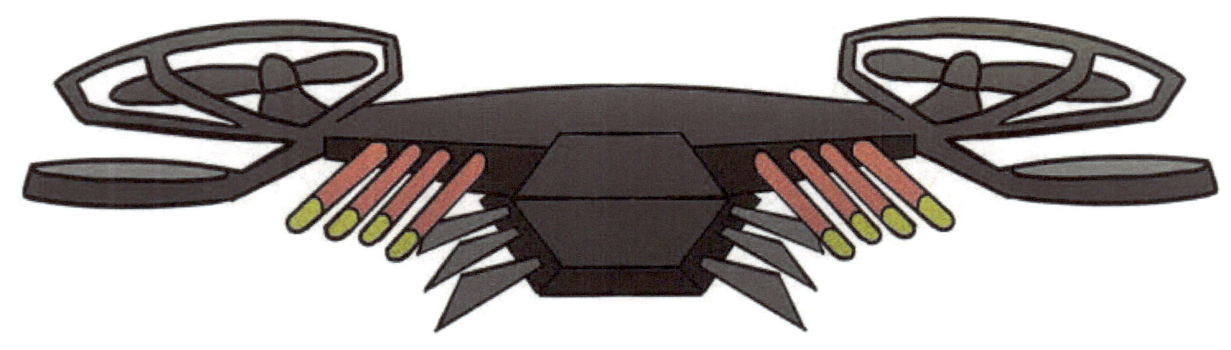

AERIAL SPIDER DRONE
SURFACE TO SURFACE MISSILES
RETRACTABLE SPIDER LEGS

The aerial spider drones, can go anywhere, they have spider legs also, and fly anywhere, at any height, and have powerful weapons, some are equipped with missiles, some have lasers.

Before the large groups of hostiles, can use rocket launchers, and grenades, or place IED's, the (HEL) the high energy laser towers, equipped with powerful kilowatt lasers, fire with extreme accuracy lasers at the large groups of hostiles, especially those who have rocket launchers, grenades, IED's.

Taking out entire groups, within seconds, this is followed by the assaults in the air, and in pure darkness, by many aerial spider drones, fi ring missiles, and lasers.

The Afghanistan government is observing only in a distance, to prevent friendly fire among the allies, and themselves.

SUPER SOLDIER
KILOWATT LASERS

SPIDER SUPER SOLDIER
KILOWATT LASER

The super soldiers are in position, and are equipped with massive laser weapons, only if needed.

This continues throughout the night, and after encountering the system of (HEL) high energy lasers, from each tower, and many aerial spider drones, firing nonstop missiles, and lasers.

The hostiles retreat back into the mountains, having many causalities, they regroup back in the mountains, the leaders under minded the sheer power, and mobilities, of the aerial spider drones, and the precision of the (HEL) high energy lasers on each tower.

Overall the entire system is an overwhelming success, for the first time, the program is viewed as a game changer.

After this demonstration, the world can finally view how important technological advancements are and bring real solutions to troubled regions.

The entire system, including the (HEL) high energy laser towers, aerial spider drones, ground super soldiers, and the satellites above, are all equipped with the latest in infrared technologies.

No attacks late at night by surprise, now the team of the robotic engineering program, can protect the group of engineers, and workers, at the three river basins, The Amu Darya, The Kabul, and The Helmand, plus the dams, Sorobi, Kajaki.

To allow the much needed Hydro projects, and Afghanistan can finally become HydroHegemon, increasing water productions from 17 BCM to 30 BCM, and meeting the challenges in, Biophysicist, Socioeconomic, Environmental, Hydrologic, developments, for futures to come.

The Afghanistan government will also take steps to secure peace, by recognizing the Taliban, as a legitimate political party, to bring everyone together. This success is owed to the program, the corporation of governments, leaders, tribes, and especially the team of robotic engineering scientists, and the military strategists, experts, Congressmen Chris Whitman, Director Jones, and special team.

Back in the mountains of Afghanistan, the Taliban leaders, speak to their armies of men, grabbing a hand full of red dirt, and saying, defeat shall only make us stronger, for these lands are from are ancestors, generations of families, now, the Afghanistan government finally recognizes us, as a legitimate political party, and we can participate in forming a greater Afghanistan. The biggest concerns, for the program, are at the borders, and the three large river basins, and the dams, with the Hydro projects.

The Pakistan military will still guard the border on their side, away from the buffer zones, and all other parties, have witnessed the effectiveness of the entire system.

JON
TAN
LAN

SAM
ANDRE
DAME

MARCUS
JOHNSON

TIM
VON
GLEASON

RON
BEN
RUCKMAN

The team of robotic engineering scientists can be assured, that the program, can run itself, and they can monitor everything at home base, back in the states.

The team of robotic engineering scientists, will stay a little bit longer in Afghanistan, only until the Hydro projects are complete, then return for a well-deserved vacation with their families.

Months, continue to go by, and the group of engineers, and workers, are working around the clock, in the Hydro projects, everything seems to be moving forward.

Only with the exception of spontaneous group attacks around the buffer zones, from hostiles, but between the (HEL) laser towers, and the mobilities, and weaponry, of the aerial spider drones, their assaults, were quickly disrupted.

The system, and the entire program, is a force, that cannot be undermined, every attack, from the hostiles, has been met decisively with precision counter defensive.

The program, and it's system, has gone beyond the requirements, to protect, and prevent hostile attacks, in all perimeters.

After, the Hydro projects, are finally completed, the water levels increase, from 17 BCM to 30 BCM.

Now, all that's needed, is for the restoration plan (UNOP), with the agreements of all nations involved, to be honored, to insure the future of the Helmand river.

The team of robotic engineering scientists, and the (DARPA) program, are a huge success.

Now, the team can return back to the states, where they can monitor everything, and the United States military has a base in Afghanistan also.

With the success of the (DARPA) program, the military personnel can be greatly reduced, and the Afghanistan government can finally make progress, to better the conditions in Afghanistan.

The team returns by military plane, back to the states, where everyone is waiting for them, including family, Congressman Chris Whitman, Director Jones, etc.

Once they land, the team reunites with everyone, and quickly, Congressman Chris Whitman, and Director Jones, make an announcement.

This gathering has a catering service with drinks, and food, even some shows for the kids.

The announcement is made, let us toast to the future of the (DARPA) program, and it's success, we have brought the future to Afghanistan, and are currently working on other missions.

May God be with the United States of America, and it's allies, and the (DARPA) program, solving extraordinary problems, throughout our world, eliminating human soldier casualties, for futures to come.

Everyone, after the speech started clapping, and after the luncheon, the team of robotic engineering scientists, returned home, to be with their families for six months, with some security detail, for a well deserved vacation.

After the success of the (DARPA) program, future missions, shall be carefully planned, and executed, but also each mission has extreme difficulties, that require time, corroboration, and many factors, to consider before moving forward.

www.ingramcontent.com/pod-product-compliance
Lightning Source LLC
Chambersburg PA
CBHW041920180726
48295CB00002B/25